MICHAEL HARDCASTLE

In the Net

MAMMOTH

First published in Great Britain 1971
by Methuen Children's Books Ltd
Paperback edition published 1974
by Magnet Paperbacks
Reprinted 1977, 1980, 1982, 1984 (twice), 1987, 1989
Published 1990 by Mammoth
an imprint of Reed Consumer Books Limited
Michelin House, 81 Fulham Road, London SW3 6RB
and Auckland, Melbourne, Singapore and Toronto

Reprinted 1990, 1991, 1992 (twice), 1993 (twice)

ISBN 0 7497 0426 8

A CIP catalogue record for this title
is available from the British Library

Text copyright © 1971 by Michael Hardcastle
Illustrations copyright © 1971
by Methuen Children's Books Ltd
Printed and bound in Great Britain
by Cox & Wyman Ltd, Reading, Berkshire

Illustrated by Trevor Stubley

One

As the ball bounced gently on the turf Gary Ansell trapped it under his studs. Quickly he rolled it forward with the side of his boot. No one was in a position for a pass. They hadn't expected him to get the ball. He began to run with it.

A defender came at him. Gary slipped past him easily, still looking for a team-mate. Then Mickey Swift yelled for a pass. Gary pushed the ball to him with the inside of his right foot. But Swift didn't live up to his name. He was much too slow to take the pass. The ball went over the by-line for a goal-kick.

"You're too slow to catch cold," Gary told Mickey. It was a phrase Gary's mother used when he was late home for his tea.

"Wasn't my fault," Mickey replied hotly. "You didn't hit it hard enough."

Gary didn't argue. He just wanted to get on with the game.

A few minutes later he had a shot at goal. The ball whizzed past the goalkeeper. But it hit the pile of jackets being used as a post.

"It's in the net!" Gary yelled. The rest of his team agreed with him. But the other side said it wasn't a goal. If it had been a real post the ball would have bounced back into play.

The game stopped while the row went on. Nobody was winning the argument. They needed a referee. But this was just a kick-about on the spare ground behind the avenue. To Gary, however, it was just as important as a real game.

At that moment Rex Toler pointed at the sky. "Hey, look," he called. So everyone looked up. "That's the new Russian jet," he told them. Rex was mad on planes. He always heard them before anyone else did. At school even the masters called him Pilot.

"Oh, come on!" Gary said. The players took no notice. They were listening to Rex. He was as

6

good as a visit to the airport. There was nothing he couldn't tell them about the various planes that took off or landed.

Gary began to kick the ball about on his own. He was mad at the other players. They just didn't *care*. It was almost as bad at his new school, Scale Hill Comprehensive. They did play soccer there but it wasn't the top game; that was rugby. Even athletics was more popular than soccer with some people. That was because Mr Mordant, the headmaster, was a fanatic about running. "Run, boy, *run*", he would say when a boy left his office.

The older boys said that Old Mordy was keen on athletics because he used to be a runner himself. Somebody had heard that he even ran in the Olympic Games. But Rob Roy Stuart killed that idea. "The Olympics hadn't started when Old Mordy was a young man," he said.

Nobody argued with Rob Roy. He could beat any boy in the school—even those bigger than himself.

Gary was fed up with the dispute about his goal. "Okay, okay, it wasn't a goal," he told the other players. Luckily the Russian jet was now out of sight. So the game began again. It was agreed to re-start with a free kick. That was against the rules. But Gary didn't mind so long as they were all playing instead of talking.

It was some time before the ball came his way. So anxious was he to get into action that he misjudged the bounce of the ball. He caught the ball with his knee instead of his foot and it flicked upwards on to his chest.

"Foul! Hand ball!" yelled Kevin Ripley, a small, dark-haired boy who was playing in the other team. He was a good player but he always liked to get his own way; sometimes he tried the odd trick that was outside the laws of the game.

"Rubbish! The ball hit my chest," Gary replied. "That's fair enough. You want your eyes testing."

Once again the game had come to a halt. Gary's team supported him, Kevin's side demanded a free kick.

"Come on, play the game," Kevin said to Gary. "If you can't win by fair means don't start committing fouls. That's what my dad says about Villa. They're just like you, Ansell."

8

Gary was furious. In a moment, he knew, he'd lose his temper. That was always happening when he was angry. He wanted to hit somebody; he wanted to hit Kevin now, both for the things he'd said and for spoiling the game.

At home he used to lose his temper quite regularly. When something went badly wrong he came to the boil like a kettle; he just had to let off steam, so he opened his mouth—and sometimes said terrible things.

"You must learn to control your temper," his mother told him. "Otherwise you'll end up in a lot of trouble. Count up to ten slowly—*before you say anything*. Then you'll be in control of yourself."

Now, as he and Kevin faced each other, Gary mentally began counting. He'd got up to six when Kevin broke the silence.

"Lost for words, Ansell? That proves you're in the wrong. So get out the way while I take this free kick."

Gary reached nine, then he exploded. "NO! It WASN'T a foul! You're not having a free...."

But he was too late. Ripley had placed the ball

9

and swung his foot. His team was already on the attack again.

Gary felt cheated. The count-up-to-ten control system worked sometimes—and sometimes it didn't. He felt it had failed this time, even though he'd managed to keep his temper in check. It was just that Kevin had taken advantage of it.

That unfair free kick actually led to a goal—for Kevin's side. The ball was swept quite expertly across the field. The winger centred it. The goalkeeper tried to punch the ball clear but missed it completely. Ripley himself was in just the right position to stop the ball and then prod it between the posts.

Kevin's gleeful shouts echoed round the houses and his team-mates mobbed him. At least, thought Gary, they're now showing some enthusiasm for the match. Ripley's side was leading 2-1 and Gary felt sick about it all. He hated to lose even a friendly game. What made things worse in this instance was that Kevin's goal would never have been allowed by a referee. Ripley was clearly off-side when he scored.

"That'll teach you to commit rotten fouls," Kevin sneered at Gary as he jogged back to the centre-circle. Gary made no reply. He knew Kevin was only trying to provoke him into losing his temper.

From the kick-off the ball came quickly to Gary. He moved forward smartly, evading two lunging tackles, and took the ball up the field. The defenders began to drop back. No one came in to challenge him. Gary was able to take his time and he looked for a team-mate in a good position. Then he spotted Tommy Saxton on his own on the other side of the field. No defender appeared to be watching him.

12

Gary gave a huge kick at the ball and yelled, "Tommy! It's yours!"

It was a perfect pass but it was wasted on Tommy Saxton: he wasn't even looking at the ball. All he was interested in was his wristwatch. He was studying that with all the concentration that Gary would give to the FA Cup Final. He had received it the previous day as a birthday present.

"It's precisely 5.55," he announced importantly. "I'm off for my tea now. S'long."

The ball bounced just in front of him and Tommy didn't even notice it. He always thought more of his stomach than anything else.

"Oh, no!" Gary yelled in disgust. "You can't stop now!"

"I can—and I have," Tommy retorted smugly. "Nothing keeps me away from my tea when it's ready."

Tommy's sister, Jenny, who was in Gary's class at Scale Hill often said that Tommy ate enough food for three boys. Luckily, she had a small appetite (or so she said. Gary, having seen the stuff she brought to school, wasn't so sure).

13

Tommy's departure was the signal for two other boys to decide it was time they went, too. The game was in danger of coming to an early end. Hurriedly Gary collected the ball from over the by-line. He tossed it to the goalkeeper.

"Kick it out," he said. "The game's not over yet."

All the same, it didn't last much longer. One by one the players drifted away to their homes. Gary managed to score a goal but there wasn't much satisfaction in it. The opposing team had lost more players than his own.

"Come on, let's pack it in," Kevin Ripley said. "It's a draw now so that's fair."

It was, really, but Gary wasn't going to admit it. All along he'd been confident his side had the beating of Ripley's. Now he'd have nothing to boast about when they met at school the next day. With Ripley's team having won the previous match earlier in the week Gary had wanted revenge.

He toed the ball to Gary, who owned it. They picked up their coats, the last two in the pile; and so the goal-posts disappeared.

"Going to watch Albion on Saturday?" Kevin asked as they strolled from the field.

"Hope so. But, well, I'm not dead sure I'll be able to get there."

"What! But they're playing United, the League leaders. Only a corpse would miss that match."

"It's my mother that's the trouble." Gary saw Kevin's eyes rolling upwards and hastened to explain. "She wants me to have some new shoes, you see. Says I keep ruining the ones I've got. And Ray, my brother, he works in a shoe shop and can get new shoes at a reduced price. They've just got some new stock in—so that's where I've got to go. Deadly, isn't it?"

"You can go in the morning, can't you? I mean, Albion are more important than *any*-thing."

"I know. But she says the morning's for shop-ping—getting in the weekend food from the village. She usually wants me to help with that as well. I never have a minute to call my own, honestly."

"I'll come round for you at two o'clock," Kevin said. "I'll tell her I've got tickets. She won't know the difference. Anyway, if your brother works in the shop you can get shoes at any time."

That's what Gary thought as well. It occurred to him that Kevin Ripley could be quite human at times. He'd be not bad at all if he didn't commit so many dirty fouls.

They parted at the entrance to Kevin's home without any farewells. It was almost as if Ripley, a year older than Gary, didn't want to be seen associating with a younger boy. The odd thing was that he was the smaller by at least an inch. At the moment they were friendly enough to each other; at school it was quite likely they'd be quarrelling again.

Gary dribbled the ball along the pavement, occasionally flicking it against a wall or a gate-post and trapping the rebound. At one point a yapping poodle came rushing down a path to tackle England's newest and youngest inter-national winger—Gary's current dream role. But the England player was too fleet-footed for the poodle; he hammered the ball upfield to his centre-forward and gave chase himself. After all, the centre-forward might make a hash of the pass.

Then it would be Gary who had the best chance of scoring.

With a neat swerve he took the ball through the gate of his own home and then steadied himself for a shot at goal. The garage doors were wide open, which meant that his father wasn't home yet. Gary aimed for the angle of the corner at the back of the garage. He hit the ball hard with his right foot: and then wished he'd used his left, because that was the weaker. The ball smacked into the concrete only inches away from the target. It bounced back against the hand-supports of the old lawn-mower before coming to rest by a petrol can. Once Gary had knocked that can over when it was half full of fuel. That week he lost his pocket money.

Satisfied that not a better goal could have been scored by *anyone*, he went into the house. As always, his mother was doing something in the kitchen. She heard him come in and called out to him. He carefully wiped the toes of his shoes on the back of his socks; he thought they didn't look too bad. He walked into the kitchen.

"Been playing football, I suppose," his mother

said, without looking up from the cooker. Gary thought he could detect the aroma of a shepherd's pie. The school lunch had been rotten.

"We did have a kick-about, yes," Gary admitted grudgingly. "Just a few of the lads."

She swung round sharply to examine his shoes. It was an old routine and he knew it by heart. What she said always depended on her mood.

"Well, they don't look too bad for once," Mrs Ansell conceded. So she must have had a good day: no headaches or dizzy spells. That was a relief to her younger son. Anyway, the pitch had been firm and grassy so there was no mud to make things worse.

"Oh, so I won't have to get any new shoes tomorrow?" Gary said, taking a chance. He should have known better.

"Indeed, you will! You get through shoes faster than—than a tramp."

"Tramps keep their shoes for years," Gary informed her. "They tie them up with bits of string and use cardboard for new soles."

"Don't be cheeky," his mother said, but not harshly. "I'm not having any son of mine looking

18

like a tramp. So you and I are going to Ray's shop tomorrow for a new pair—and if you play football in *them* you'll get no pocket money for the rest of the year. And I mean that, Gary. A whole year."

"Yes, all right," Gary said, wanting to sound helpful. "But we don't have to go in the afternoon, do we? I mean, we could manage it in the morning—if I help you with your shopping."

"My goodness, what's come over you—*offering* to help." Her look of surprise was genuine. "What is it you want to do in the afternoon, then?"

"Watch Albion."

"Well, you'll have to ask your father about that. I doubt if he'll approve. But I suppose if you're watching you won't be damaging your shoes by playing."

"We can go to the shop in the morning then? Thanks—I mean, *thanks*, Mum."

The roar of her husband's car as Godfrey Ansell turned into the drive caused Mrs Ansell to return to the cooker. Like Tommy Saxton, Mr Ansell didn't like to be kept waiting for his food. He was a big man, weighing over fifteen stone, and must have been a power in the rugby team for which he once played.

"Come on," he'd say to his wife at meal times, "let's scrum down in the dining-room." He meant he was eager to tackle his food.

When Gary had washed he went into the dining-room and was hardly through the door when a heavy cushion slammed into his midriff. He was so surprised he failed to catch it.

His father, who'd thrown it at him, laughed heartily.

"Never make a three-quarter out of you, lad, if you can't take a soft pass like that," he grinned.

"I don't want to be a three-quarter," Gary said quietly. "It's not my game. I'm going. . . ."

"Rugby'll make a man of you. It's a man's game. Soccer is for softies. With your speed you'd make a cracking three-quarter—provided you learned how to take a pass."

This was not the moment to ask permission to watch Albion, but Gary had no option. As soon as he'd finished his meal Mr Ansell would be off to his club. Gary wouldn't see him again that evening. In the morning, his father would be playing golf.

He waited until Mr Ansell was about to start on his pie. Like Gary's mother, he was a person of moods. This time, his reply to Gary's question was surprisingly mild.

"You want your head looking at if you want to watch soccer," he said. "Those players act just like silly kids when a goal's scored—hugging and kissing each other. Makes you sick to see it."

"But I'm helping mother with the shopping in the morning," Gary put in quickly.

"Oh, are you? Oh, well—perhaps just this once then. But it's not going to become habit, Gary. Remember that."

What Gary didn't know was that his father had been feeling guilty about the shopping. Mrs Ansell had asked him to help with it, for once, and he wanted to play golf instead.

"Oh, thanks, Dad, *thanks*. Albion'll eat United tomorrow. We'll absolutely *devour* them."

Two

Gary was still thinking about Dave Archer's equalizing goal for Albion against United when he made his way to the far end of the common late on Sunday afternoon. It had been an exciting match, but not a great one. Albion had attacked strongly throughout the first half but they couldn't get a goal. Gary, and the rest of the big crowd, had urged them on with everything they had. The noise was tremendous. But Albion had all the bad luck that was going; the ball just wouldn't go into the net for them.

Then, in a breakaway just after half-time, United scored. Gary wasn't alone in thinking that the goal shouldn't have been allowed. Macey, the United centre-forward, had clearly handled the ball as he brought it under control. Seemingly, the referee didn't see the incident. No wonder one section of the crowd kept telling him he was blind or needed some glasses. Even then, Macey was still in luck. His first shot was half-saved by the goalkeeper. The ball spun back to Macey who was able to flick it into the net. Gary joined in the jeering when the referee refused to listen to the Albion protests.

Only when Dave Archer scored did Gary begin to feel happy again. Up till then he'd been thinking of what his father would say if United won. Mr Ansell never missed a chance to make cheap cracks about Albion. He thought they were smart and clever and funny, but he was the only one who laughed at them. Gary just said "Ha! Ha!" very sarcastically. He rather liked doing that.

Dave Archer was Gary's private hero. He was young, a very fast winger with a powerful shot and always in the game. He'd go back to defend in his own goalmouth when the pressure was on. If anyone was injured Dave would take over in the injured man's position. He was a great player. Some of the crowd said he held on to the ball too long. But Gary knew why Dave did that: it was to give his colleagues time to get into position. Dave could centre the ball beautifully.

The previous day he had saved the match for Albion. There was no doubt about that. With only two minutes to go to full-time Dave had received a pass inside his own half. He slipped a couple of tackles quite easily. He did it so casually: that was one of the great things about Dave.

Just a twist of his hips, a jerk of his shoulders—and he'd gone the other way. He made his opponents look foolish. That was one of the reasons Dave got battered quite a lot in almost every match. Sometimes two defenders came at once. One went for the ball, the other for Dave. The young winger received a lot of bruises, but he gained plenty of free-kicks for Albion.

Gary brought his mind back to the way the goal had been scored. As he crossed the half-way line Dave had accelerated like a sports car. Yes, it was just as if he'd found an extra gear. Dave went outside the full-back and then immediately cut inside again. He left the full-back sprawling on the turf. From the very edge of the penalty area he hit the ball like a hammer striking a bullet in a gun.

It was, as the local paper reported that evening, a goal all the way. The ball flew into the top corner of the net. It went in so fast the goalkeeper never had a chance to move to it. The net bulged and Gary roared. In their relief and delight Dave's team-mates mobbed him. Gary thought it was a good thing his father wasn't there to see it.

Now, as he reached the end of the common where the trees were, Gary wondered if he'd ever score a goal as good as Dave's. He'd once read in a sports annual that Dave had practised for hours by hitting the ball against the trunk of a tree. The ball would rebound at various angles. However awkward those angles were Dave aimed to reach the ball as it shot back. He would then fire it at a target, usually another tree trunk. That way, he became a two-footed player with the ability to hit a ball from different positions.

To Gary, that seemed a very useful trick indeed. It was one that could help him personally to strengthen his shooting with his left foot. Now he found a beech tree with a fairly knobbly trunk. A few feet to the right of it and just behind it was another beech with an even broader trunk. They were exactly what he wanted.

Stripping off the blue track-suit which had been his best birthday present, he did a few loosening up exercises. This corner of the common was deserted. He didn't like to have anyone watching in case he made mistakes. Carefully he placed the ball on the ground about five yards from the first beech. He took aim and then hit the ball as hard as he could with his right foot.

The ball smacked against the bark and came back to Gary almost in a straight line. Without attempting to trap it, he slammed it towards the other tree. This time it shot back at an awkward angle and he had to sprint to reach it again.

For about half an hour he kept up this shooting practice. It meant a lot of running and was hard work. Because it was impossible to predict how the ball would rebound from the trees his reactions had to be very fast after every shot. He was sweating a lot and needed a rest. As the ball bounced back to him he killed it with his instep. Then, with a sigh of relief, he lay down on the grass. He stretched himself out and began to relax his muscles. As he lay there he watched the clouds drifting across the pale blue sky.

"Not a bad effort," said a voice somewhere above him. "But your left foot's not as good as your right, is it?"

Gary sat straight up, startled. He saw a boy of about his own age dressed in a red-and-white football shirt and white shorts; his socks were rolled down to his ankles in the style of Billy Bremner. Under his left arm he held a polka-dot football. His fair hair was cut very short and he was smiling with his eyes as well as with his mouth.

"Who're you?" Gary wanted to know. He was still surprised he'd not heard the boy approach.

"My name's Keith Nash. I'm twelve. How old are you?"

"Nearly twelve," Gary answered automatically. "Have you been spying on me? Because I don't like spies."

"I wasn't spying. Just watching, that's all. I saw you...."

"You must have been spying because I didn't see *you*. Where were you? You'd no right to spy on me like that."

Gary jumped to his feet. It wasn't so easy to argue with someone when you were sitting down and they were standing up.

"Hey, there's no need to get mad about it," Keith said quietly. "I was interested in what you were doing, that's all. It's a good way of practising, isn't it? Dave Archer used to do it."

28

Gary didn't know whether to be pleased or sorry that this other boy also knew of Dave Archer's old training method. It wasn't something Gary really wanted to share with anyone else.

"How did you know that?" he asked, although he knew the answer.

"Oh, Dave told me about it," Keith replied in the same quiet voice. He didn't sound as if he was boasting.

"He *told* you! Don't you mean you read about it in a book?"

"No. He told me when he came to give a talk at our school. He's an old boy of Bankside Grammar—that's where I go. Actually, we had quite a good chat. I told him about the team I captain in the Sunday Junior League. He was very interested. Said he'd come and watch us one day. I bet he will, too. He's a great guy, is Dave Archer. It was a super goal he scored yesterday. I wish the television cameras had been there. It might have won the Goal-of-the-Season Award. But now it won't count because it wasn't on television."

Gary felt much the same. But there was no one

29

he could have discussed it with at home; and there were few boys in his class at Scale Hill who were real Albion supporters. Already he was beginning to like Keith Nash.

One thing, however, worried Gary: that Keith was a pupil at Bankside Grammar School. There was supposed to be some rivalry between Scale Hill and Bankside, but Gary had not been at his new school long enough to see much evidence of it.

"I go to Scale Hill," Gary said and waited to see what reaction this would bring from Keith. All it brought was a bigger grin.

"Hard lines," Keith said sympathetically. "You haven't got much of a soccer team there, have you? Your lot plays too much rugby. *We* gave up that stupid game years ago. It's so—so *ancient*.

"Look," he went on, "would you like to play for us next Sunday? We'll give you a try-out and if you fit in—well, maybe you could play for us regularly. We have some great games in the League. We haven't lost yet. Won two, drawn two."

Gary was elated. But he didn't want to appear

too eager; and, anyway, he didn't know how good the other players were.

"What's the name of your team?"

"Bank Vale United. Four of us go to Bankside and four go to Moss Vale Secondary. Now we're united, see?" Keith was grinning again.

"What about the others?"

"Oh, they're just friends—no regulars. Actually, we're a bit short of players at the moment. Not everybody can get off on a Sunday afternoon. There's always some stinking homework to do. D'you get much?"

"Sometimes. It just depends. But I usually do it on Sunday morning."

"Wish I could. But my mother makes me go to chapel with her. Waste of good football training time. Look, what's your favourite position in the team?"

"Right wing."

"Yes, I thought it might be. Well, if you turn out half as good as Dave you'll be all right with us. By the way, what's your name?"

Gary told him and then they began to walk across the common together. After a few yards

Keith drop-kicked his ball as far as he could ahead of them and they both gave chase. For the rest of the way to the end of the common they ran and exchanged passes. Gary, who was so used to training on his own, found it great fun to have a companion. He got the impression that Keith was a very useful player indeed. He was particularly good at trapping a ball.

"I've been thinking," Gary said as they turned into the avenue where he lived. "If you're short of players for United I could ask a pal of mine if he'd like to turn out. He's not bad."

He was thinking of Kevin Ripley (and trying not to think of some of the fouls that Ripley committed). When Kevin wasn't being selfish he could be a very good player; he was always better to play with than against.

"Okay," nodded Keith, "if he's any good. If we can get a settled team we can win this League. The winners get medals and a trophy. Oh, and Dave Archer said he'd give us some kit as well— so long as we win."

"That'd be great! Look, where shall I see you next Sunday?" asked Gary. "And what time?"

Keith explained the arrangements and then they parted. Gary would have liked to tell them about it at home, but he knew it would be a dangerous topic to mention. His father and mother might well be united against him playing soccer on a Sunday. The story would have to wait until he saw Kevin Ripley later in the week. Meanwhile, it was good to think about it just by himself.

One of the best things about Mondays was that the double sports period for Gary's class was held at the end of the afternoon. So far the boys had not had any organized games of either soccer or rugby; instead, they'd practised together in small groups for whichever game they preferred.

On the day following Gary's meeting with Keith the sports master, Mr Moore, divided the boys into two teams, one of eleven players, the other of fifteen. To his alarm Gary found himself among the fifteen. The last thing he wanted to do was to play rugby. In unison with a boy called Langford, a keen Albion fan, he tried to protest.

"In this life," Mr Moore said, cutting them

33

short, "you can't always have what you want. You have to learn to do some things you think you might not like. And you never know, after you've tried them you might begin to like them. So it's rugby training for you today."

Langford's mouth twisted in disappointment.

"Now don't start sulking," Mr Moore said sharply. "If you're going to act like a spoilt child you'll have no games at all for the rest of the term. Understand?"

"Yes, sir," Langford said dutifully.

"Good," said Mr Moore, picking up a rugby ball. He lobbed it at Gary who caught it instinctively. It was easier to catch than the hard cushions his father so often hurled at him unexpectedly.

The sports master led them across to the rugby pitch where another team of boys in Gary's age-group was waiting with one of Mr Moore's colleagues. Sadly, Gary noted that the boys from his class who'd been selected for soccer were about to start their game.

Mr Moore briskly organized a team and picked Gary as a wing three-quarter. "I had reports from

34

your junior school that you're quite a fair sprinter, Ansell. So let's see how fast you can go down the wing when you get the ball. We could do with a speed merchant in the Junior Fifteen."

It was not long after the kick-off before Gary received the ball. He took the pass cleanly and set off for the corner flag. When a boy came to tackle him he dummied automatically and went past him with no trouble.

His opposing winger began to give chase but Gary was much too speedy for him. Evading another tackle, Gary looked for someone to pass to, but none of his team-mates had kept up with

him. So Gary was forced to continue on his own.

Another opponent who'd never attempted to tackle anyone in his life loomed up in his path but Gary was able to brush him aside. Now there was no one between him and the try-line and, thankfully, he dived over it.

It was only when he started to pick himself up that he realized what he'd done. He'd scored a try the very first time he'd touched the ball in a game of rugby.

"Well done, well done!" enthused Mr Moore as he ran up like a referee to mark the score. "You really have got a turn of foot and no mistake. If you can keep this up we'll make a proper rugby player out of you. My goodness, yes."

Gary could only stare at him, open-mouthed. The one thing he wanted to say he dare not say —not at this moment. He could imagine Mr Moore's anger if he told him now that he hated rugby, that all he wanted to do was to play soccer.

His team-mates called out their congratulations, but Gary didn't hear them as he trudged back to the half-way line. He was staring across the field at the boys enjoying their soccer.

Three

There was excitement in the air. It was so powerful Gary felt he could reach out and actually
touch it. Instead, he stripped off his track-suit and
fingered the green shirt he was wearing. It didn't
bear the figure "7" or any number at all. But it
was his first real team shirt. Where Keith Nash
had got the shirts for his team Gary didn't know.
He just accepted now that Keith knew how to
arrange things.

From among school friends and acquaintances
he'd organized a soccer team, Bank Vale United.
He'd organized their entry into the Sunday Junior
League, their fixtures, their kit, even some supporters. Only the excitement before the start of
the match had developed naturally.

All morning—and for most of the previous

week, come to that—Gary had thought of little else but his first game for the team. When Gary had mentioned the subject to him, Kevin Ripley had displayed immediate interest. "Just the job," he'd said. "I need some regular practice." Gary had pointed out that they'd be playing in a real competition, not practice matches, but Kevin ignored that. He was thinking of himself, not the team.

As he limbered up on the touch-line Gary glanced across at Kevin who was talking away to Keith Nash. For one who was himself so used to talking, Keith seemed to be a good listener. Gary wondered what they were discussing.

In a way, it wasn't fair. After all, he, Gary, had introduced the two boys to each other. If they were already discussing tactics for the match then they should have consulted him and the other members of the team. Feeling a bit shut out, he wandered across to them. They were so deep in conversation they didn't even look at him.

"Got everything sorted out?" he asked eventually.

"Oh, sure," Kevin answered confidently. "You

just play your normal game, boyo, and leave the rest to us. I reckon we know how to sort out this Hollow Lane mob. You just stay out on your wing."

"Thanks very much," Gary replied. He meant it to sound sarcastic, but if it did Kevin took no notice. With one arm round Keith's shoulders he was leading the way to the centre-circle. Unhappily, Gary followed them. The referee, a senior boy from a local school, strolled importantly on to the field and then blew a long blast on his whistle.

Keith and the opposing captain of Hollow Lane Rovers solemnly shook hands and Keith, on winning the toss, chose to play against the slight slope of the pitch. This meant conditions should be easier for United in the second half if they were feeling a bit tired.

Rovers, dressed in a variety of blue shirts began like a massed start of high-powered racing cars. The centre-forward booted the ball upfield from the kick-off and most of his team charged after it. There were some hefty boys among them and with the slope in their favour they were eager for quick goals. Lugard, their tall inside-right, tried a shot from outside the penalty area and it was only just wide of the post. Gary sensed that it was going to be a hard match.

For several minutes he was never nearer than thirty yards to the ball. Standing on the halfway line, waiting for a pass or a loose ball, he was beginning to feel both lonely and chilled. A steady rain had been falling since mid-morning and now it suddenly became much heavier. Already there was a fair amount of mud on the pitch.

He still hadn't touched the ball when Rovers scored. Lugard, who seemed to be everywhere, won a corner on the right wing. The centre was a good one to the edge of the area. One of United's full-backs missed his kick, the ball was pushed towards the penalty spot where Lugard was waiting to ram it into the net.

Depressed, the United players trooped back to their positions. Kevin was saying something quickly to Keith who just shook his head.

"No," Gary heard him say, "if you get mad at a bloke he'll probably make some more mistakes. Forget it."

"Rubbish," Kevin said. "You're the captain. You should have told that idiot full-back to watch the ball properly. You should have sharpened him up, get him thinking about his job."

"Look, let's just score some goals ourselves— right?" Keith replied firmly.

To Gary's surprise, Kevin said no more. As the inside-left he received the ball from the kick-off and straightaway tried to force his way through a crowd of Rovers. When he lost the ball he flicked out his foot and tripped an opponent. Immediately the referee blew for a foul. Kevin tried to protest but the referee just waved him away.

One of the solidly-built Rovers defenders booted the ball deep into the United half of the field. Keith Nash tackled doggedly as Rovers tried to force the ball into the penalty area. By now Kevin had stopped sulking and even he had dropped back to help the defence. Gary was thinking it was about time he did something himself when Rovers scored again. Once more, it was Lugard who put the ball in the net with a fierce drive.

"Come *on*, lads, stop messing about," Kevin

41

yelled at his team-mates. "Get stuck in!"

Keith looked as if he were about to say something to Kevin, perhaps to remind him who was captain, but then he just nodded his agreement. After all, Ripley was only showing how keen he was to win the match.

Probably because they now felt that with a two-goal lead they could relax a little, Rovers fell back from the kick-off. For the first time in the match Gary touched the ball. From Keith, a wing-half who loved to start an attack, he received a gem of a pass almost on the touch-line. Two Rovers players rushed at him but Gary's speed took him past them with ease. Following instructions, he kept to his wing; that was all to the good because there the turf was drier.

As he ran he tried to watch the progress of Kevin and Harvey Slater, United's centre-forward, a tall boy with very long hair. Both boys were racing through the middle, hopeful of Gary's being able to cross the ball to them. Predictably, Kevin was soon yelling for a pass, one arm waving above his head to indicate his position.

Gary neatly tricked a defender by half-stopping

42

and then accelerating again as the boy hesitated —Dave Archer was good at that—before hitting the ball as hard as he could into the centre.

It bounced towards Ripley at knee height. He killed it swiftly with his instep, swivelled, and in the same movement crashed the ball towards the goal. In that moment he showed some of the real skill which he possessed. When he concentrated on playing the game properly instead of turning it into a private battlefield he was a fine footballer. This time, however, the goalkeeper was able to punch the ball away to a colleague who belted it into touch. It was obvious that Rovers were not a clever team: but they were big and rugged and could kick hard.

After thirty-five minutes the referee blew for half-time with Rovers still leading by Lugard's two goals. As the teams separated into two groups near the half-way line Gary heard one of their opponents say: "This lot are easy. We'll murder them in the second half."

Kevin must have heard the remark because he shouted back: "That's what you think! We haven't started yet."

It was Keith, however, who announced what their new tactics were to be. Rovers, he said, hadn't much skill, whereas United had some good ball-players. So United would keep the ball on the ground as much as possible and hope to get through the defence with close passing. Gary was to come inside more and team up with Kevin and Harvey. With the slope in their favour now they should be able to keep up a constant attack. The rest of the players nodded their agreement. Surprisingly, Kevin had no comment to make. He just listened to his captain.

"Look, we haven't lost a match yet—and we're not going to lose this one," Keith said as the referee blew for the start of the second half.

Rovers were jolted by the determination with which United resumed. Ripley began a mazy dribble deep into their half and when at last he lost the ball Gary was on hand to take it into the penalty area. A defender lurched past him as he switched the ball from one foot to the other. Ripley was calling for the ball again but Gary ignored him. By now Kevin was being closely marked. Out of the corner of his eye he saw Keith

44

Nash coming up fast to the edge of the area. Neatly Gary steered the ball into his path.

Keith didn't hesitate. He hit the ball with all the force he could muster. It sped across the penalty area, only inches above the turf. But his aim was slightly at fault: the ball was going just wide of the far post. One Rovers player, however, saw danger where none existed. He stuck out his leg to steer the ball away—and succeeded only in deflecting it into the net. No one was more surprised than the goalkeeper; he didn't even move as the ball went past him.

Kevin exploded with joy. He rushed over to Keith to slap him heartily on the back. It was the signal for the rest of the United players to congratulate their captain. Some of them hugged him. United were now only one goal in arrears.

Led by Lugard, Rovers tried desperately to restore their lead without delay. Keith, doubtless inspired by the goal, played brilliantly to keep Rovers at bay. Suddenly he burst out of a mêlée with the ball and booted it into the Rovers half. Kevin and Gary went for it together. They were concentrating on getting the ball and didn't see each other. It was Kevin who managed to keep his balance when they collided. Gary went sprawling head first in the mud.

Kevin kept going. When he had sight of goal it took a lot to stop him and most of the Rovers were still in the United half of the field. Pushing the ball ahead of him—but not too far ahead—he surged into the penalty area. The goalkeeper, unprotected by any team-mates, had been well trained. He knew he should come out to narrow the angle in such a situation. So out he came. One swerve and Kevin was round him. Then with a tremendous kick he smashed the ball into the net. He could, of course, simply have tapped it in : but that wasn't Kevin's way.

His reaction had to be seen to be believed. Having turned almost a cart-wheel, he danced halfway across the pitch, his arms waving above his head like a sword-dancer's. His colleagues showered him with praise for what was a very good goal. Only Gary was not among them—he was still trying to wipe the mud from his pants and shirt. Kevin bounced up to him.

"Hey," he said accusingly, "don't get in my

way again. You nearly stopped me scoring that goal."

He meant it—even though he was still smiling with the pleasure the equaliser had given him.

"It was the purest accident," Gary replied, using a phrase he'd heard at home many times during domestic upsets. But he wasn't going to argue with Kevin—he was just as elated by the goal as the rest of the United players were.

It proved to be the last of the match. With the rain still falling and the pitch getting muddier all the time both teams soon tired. Towards the end, few players could manage to run more than a couple of yards. Kevin, who seemed to have more energy than most in spite of his size, was still trying to grab the winner when the final whistle blew. He even accused the referee of not adding on time for injuries, though there'd been none. The rest of the players shook hands and seemed satisfied with the result.

"It was a good point to get because they were bigger and stronger than us," Keith pointed out. "And we're still unbeaten."

There was no doubt that Kevin was the hero of

48

the day. He walked off towards the common with Keith's arm round his shoulders; neither of them bothered to change. Once more Gary felt left out, but he knew he should get home as soon as possible. His mother was sure to ask where he'd been.

He hadn't had a particularly good game and he was worrying about that as he reached the door into the kitchen. He could hear his mother moving about inside and suddenly he remembered they were having visitors for tea. His aunt and uncle and cousin Lucy were coming and might even have arrived.

Cautiously he pushed open the door, hoping to creep in unnoticed, but his mother spotted him immediately.

"And where've you been?" she demanded, brushing a sleeve across her forehead. Clearly she had one of her bad heads again.

"Out," he said quietly—the wrong thing to say of course.

"I can see that, just look at you! Filthy! Mud all over you. And I told you to be back early for tea."

She stepped forward without warning and

savagely unzipped the top of his tracksuit. His shirt was even muddier.

"Just look at you, just look at you!" She was making more noise than Kevin when he scored a goal. "Well you can get those overalls off right now. This minute!"

Normally Gary would have objected to having his beloved track-suit described as overalls. Now he had the sense to keep silent. He started to take

it off. His mother's voice had carried to the sitting-room and everybody trooped into the kitchen to see what the noise was all about. Lucy was the first to arrive and stare at him. She was a few months older than Gary and he was positive she didn't like him. In her short blue polka-dot dress and with red bows in her plaits she looked prim and very clean.

He hated the idea of stripping to his pants and shirt in front of Lucy, but he daren't disobey orders—particularly as his father was now asking searching questions. His brother Ray now joined the attack, enquiring whether Gary had been playing rugby—with a round ball.

When his mother saw just how much mud he had collected she nearly had hysterics. "You can get the rest of your things off now—here in the kitchen. You're not going up my stair-carpet like that! Then you're going to have a bath, my boy, a proper scrub from head to foot."

Gary was no longer really aware of what his mother was saying. All he was conscious of was the smirk on Lucy's face. He wished he dare grab a handful of mud and plaster it all over her. She

51

wouldn't be laughing at him then.

It was his uncle who came to Gary's rescue. "Come on, Lucy, let's get back to that horsey book of yours. I want to find out what happens next." Dutifully, she returned to the sitting-room with him; she was still smirking.

One by one the other adults drifted away. When they were on their own again his mother relented a little and agreed that he could get undressed in his bedroom so long as he had his bath straightaway. As he washed the worst of the mud off his arms and legs at the kitchen sink she lectured him on the subject of politeness when guests were expected. There was a time and a place for everything but that didn't include football on Sunday afternoon.

"So just think on," she called out to him as Gary ran up the stairs, "we're not having this to-do every week."

Four

"And so, you see, that's what the Wars of the Roses were really about," said the history master. "It's a fascinating period."

Gary was one boy who didn't agree with him. To him, this sort of history, all about old battles and dates, was dead boring. A detailed account of the Football League: now *that* really would be fascinating. He'd like to know how the League was formed, which clubs were founder members and who won the very first Championship.

Not for the first time Gary's thoughts returned to the match of the previous day. It was now the third game he'd played for Bank Vale United. Although the team had won its second successive victory it wasn't one Gary would remember with much pleasure. For one thing he'd missed an open goal, for another he'd been accused of selfishness by Kevin Ripley.

After missing that easy chance of a goal Gary had done his best to hold on to the ball whenever he received a pass. He knew he could beat this defence and he wanted to cut in towards goal as often as possible to give his team-mates good opportunities to score. If United won easily it would help their goal average. But he wasn't being selfish: he was playing as hard as he could for the team. It was just that Kevin didn't see it that way—especially after one incident towards the end of the match.

Gary had won the ball from a tackle in midfield and automatically took it out to the wing. Unlike those of most boys' teams, the defence began to retreat methodically. Obviously the side was well trained even if it lacked skill. So Gary was able to make easy progress down the flank as opponents fell back before him. Both Ripley and Harvey Slater moved forward swiftly in anticipation of a pass.

As usual, Kevin started to scream for the ball. He was the noisiest player Gary had ever known.

One result of Kevin's shouting was that opponents tended to stick close to him, expecting that he was bound to receive the ball before long. Kevin didn't seem to mind this close marking; indeed, he probably revelled in it. If he escaped the traps set for him it showed what a clever player he was.

This time, however, three boys were surrounding him and Gary judged that a pass to Kevin was sure to be intercepted. With Kevin having scored two goals already the defence was not going to leave him unmarked for a moment. So Gary ignored his inside-left and continued to work the ball towards the by-line. Two or three times he gave the impression that he was going to make a pass but instead he held on to the ball.

Suddenly he realized that he himself had the best opening for a shot at goal. All the other United forwards were either closely marked or in the wrong position. He spurted past a lumbering full-back and hit the ball hard. It was right on target, but the goalkeeper reacted quickly and brought off an excellent save.

At the time Kevin didn't complain to Gary. It was as they came off the field at the end of the match that Ripley accused him of letting the side down by sticking to the ball when he should have passed it.

Gary was taken aback. He knew he'd done the right thing in shooting when he had. As he pointed out, it would've been a goal but for the goalie's lucky save (most forwards always said it was only a lucky save that prevented them from scoring).

"You'd never have had a chance," he told Kevin. "Those defenders were swarming round you like bees round a jam pot."

Ripley wasn't impressed. "I'd've easily got through them," he boasted. "I could beat them with both hands tied behind my back—and one leg in plaster."

Gary was pretty sure Kevin had pinched that phrase from a sports story but he didn't say so. Clearly Kevin felt he and the other forwards had been cheated of an easy goal by Gary's solo effort. Keith Nash seemed to agree with him.

"Look, Gary," he said, "if you don't pass the ball we can't score. You can't do it all on your own. You're not as good as Dave Archer yet. So

push the ball around a bit—don't hog it to yourself. Okay?"

Gary started to argue that he had as much right
as anyone else to have a shot at goal. Nash didn't
want to listen, though he always listened to anything Kevin had to say. Because Kevin made so
much fuss about everything, it seemed to Gary
that Keith always took Kevin's side. Keith just
caved in under Kevin's blustering.

"Look," he said, cutting Gary off in mid-
sentence, "I'm the captain. What I say goes. So
play for the team—not for yourself. Otherwise...."

He said no more but left his threat hanging in
the air like a dark cloud. Gary was furious. Nobody played harder for the team than he did. It
was so rotten and unfair to say that he was playing for himself. There was not much point in
counting up to ten this time because already Keith
had wandered off—as usual with his arm round
Ripley's shoulders. These days they were insepar-
able. If you met one of them you were sure to
meet the other as well. It was a wonder Keith

hadn't invited Kevin to share the captaincy with him.

Gary's black mood began to lift during Monday afternoon as the clock moved round towards 2.40 and the start of the double games period. He was eager to get out on the football field. It was so stuffy in the classrooms.

When they assembled on the sports ground, however, he was dismayed to find himself among the rugby group.

"But, sir," he objected to Mr Moore, "I played rugby last week."

"Quite right, Ansell. You've got a good memory." Mr Moore favoured a little sarcasm. "And you did very well. You might make a useful rugger player one day—if you get down to it. Now...."

"But, sir, it's my turn for soccer this week! That's only fair."

"Ansell, as you get a bit older you'll discover that life can be *very* unfair. You'll just have to learn to put up with it."

"But, sir...."

"Ansell, you've said that already, three times.

If you say it again you'll find yourself back in the changing-room immediately. So I'd shut up if I were you."

There was no arguing in the face of such a rebuff—and such a threat—and Gary retreated to the edge of the group. He knew that Mr Moore would be watching him closely throughout the game and if Gary dropped a pass or did anything stupid the sports master would say he'd done it on purpose: that he was sulking. So he'd have to play as well as he could to keep out of trouble.

Once the game started he managed to find some enjoyment in it: not much, but some. After all, he was running about in the open air on a sports field instead of being chained to a desk in a classroom. There was some fun in kicking for touch, in racing towards the try-line, even in tackling hard. Soon he knew he was having as good a game as anyone.

"Keep it up, Ansell, you're doing well—go *on*, go for the line, there's an opening to your right," Mr Moore, running hard to keep up with play, yelled at him.

Gary had already seen his chance of a break-

59

through on the left and now he hesitated, uncertain which direction to take. The delay was fatal. Lawson, one of the biggest boys on the other side and a very good runner, came tearing up to tackle Gary. He came in like a battering ram and Gary, off-balance, was flattened. The ball slipped from his grasp and out of his reach, like a tablet of soap in the bath.

Instinctively, Gary tried to retrieve it on his hands and knees. Lawson, now on his feet again, also tried to grab the ball. In doing so, he trod heavily on Gary's ankle.

The pain was terrible. It was so bad that for several moments Gary didn't know where he was; everything seemed to have vanished in a black cloud. Tears were in his eyes and he felt very sick. Automatically, he tried to stand up, but that only increased the pain. He lay back on the turf, his hands over his eyes, one leg drawn up.

He felt hands touching him and then the voice of Mr Moore.

"All right, Ansell, all right—you're not dead yet."

Like other sports masters in Gary's experience,

Mr Moore had no sympathy for anyone. Injuries were always minor, pain never lasted long. But he hadn't had his ankle trodden on. Gary, as his brain cleared a little, was positive it was broken. He wouldn't be able to walk or kick a ball again.

He squirmed as hands fluttered over the injured places. A couple of boys were holding him down.

"No, there's nothing broken," Mr Moore said calmly. "Just bad bruising. It'll swell up a bit and you'll have to rest it. You'll soon be as right as rain, Ansell."

Gary was much less confident. He still felt sick and the pain was still pretty awful. He had to be helped off the pitch to lie down for a bit. Lawson came over and was full of apologies. He kept saying that it was an accident, a pure accident; and so it was. But that didn't really help Gary to feel any better. What he was thinking about now was whether he'd be fit for the next Sunday League game.

A few minutes later Mr Moore went over to Gary to ask him how he was feeling now.

"A bit grim, sir," Gary murmured. The injury

61

wasn't *quite* as painful as it had been, but it was bad enough.

At that moment a boy dashed up with Mr Moore's first aid box, marked with a red cross on a white circle, which he kept in his room. Gary hadn't even been aware that a boy had been sent for the box.

The sports master removed Gary's boot and sock and then rubbed some foul-smelling liniment on to a special bandage. This bandage he then bound very tightly round Gary's ankle. It was a painful business and it brought tears to Gary's eyes again.

"Now, that'll bring out the bruise and help the trouble to clear up quickly," Mr Moore said. "You'll have to rest your ankle as much as you can. You'll soon be okay again. Injuries at your age are soon mended."

At the end of the sports period Gary had to be assisted back to the changing-room, but he managed to get dressed by himself. He could just manage to walk but each step sent a throb of pain through his ankle. To Gary's surprise, Mr Moore was now very sympathetic. He even gave

Gary a lift home in his own car. Gary was a bit embarrassed by that because the boys in his class joked that he was now obviously the master's pet. They ignored the fact that he was injured.

"See how you feel tomorrow and don't come to school if it still hurts a lot," Mr Moore said as he dropped Gary off outside his home. "But it should be much better after a night's rest."

From his father, later in the evening, Gary had to put up with some more jokes. Mr Ansell, how-

ever, was more sympathetic when he learned that the accident had occurred when Gary was playing rugby.

"Oh well," he said, "you'll have to get used to being tackled. When you learn how to fall you won't get hurt. I used to get lots of knocks but I survived."

Gary's mother showed rather more concern and insisted he went to bed straight after his tea. For once, Gary didn't object: he was glad of the chance to rest his ankle. The discomfort didn't actually keep him awake but he didn't sleep very well that night.

The following day he limped to school although his mother wanted him to stay at home. His ankle still gave him some pain but gradually it felt easier. By Friday he had taken the bandage off. The bruise was a nasty one but, in a way, he was quite proud of it. Some professional soccer players, he'd been told, had permanent bruises on their legs.

That evening he decided he must try his ankle out by kicking a ball. It was the only way to find out whether he'd be fit for Sunday's match.

Gently, he dribbled a ball down the avenue. To his delight, everything seemed all right.

He'd reckoned without their neighbour's black poodle. Without warning it shot out of a gate towards him, barking furiously. Automatically, Gary swerved to avoid it. He twisted sharply on his ankle—and pain flared through it again. In that moment Gary knew he had no hope at all of playing soccer on Sunday.

Five

Even the recorded highlights on television of one of the previous day's top First Division matches couldn't hold Gary's attention on Sunday afternoon. All the time his mind kept drifting to the game that would be taking place at that moment on the common between Bank Vale United and Beltisham Wanderers.

He was wondering who had been picked to take his place on the right wing. Now that they were having so much success United were not short of boys who wanted to play for them. Just before the previous match Keith Nash had joked that soon there would be keen competition for places in the side. At least, Gary had assumed it was a joke. Perhaps, though, Keith had been serious and everyone *had* to play for his place. But Gary couldn't imagine that Keith or Kevin

Ripley would ever step down for anyone else; they were the hub of the team.

Half of Gary's mind wanted his replacement on the wing to do well, so that United would win and keep their unbeaten record; the other half rather hoped that the boy would play badly so that they would all miss Gary and be eager for him to return to the side.

Because he'd had to stay indoors since Friday Gary hadn't had a chance to see Keith or Kevin to discuss the match with them—or even to let them know that he wouldn't be playing. His mother had forbidden him to leave the house for his ankle was still swollen and painful.

Once again he was wearing a bandage and he was supposed to rest his leg as much as possible. The twist he'd give his ankle when avoiding the poodle wouldn't have mattered much if the old injury had cleared up by then. As it was, his ankle had still been a bit weak and so now his recovery would take longer. Gary decided he hated all dogs, especially poodles.

His mother had protested when he'd got up that morning after breakfast, but Gary couldn't bear to stay in bed another minute. He'd read all the football reports in the Sunday papers and he'd done his homework on Saturday afternoon (when normally he might have been watching Albion).

Now, he was bored. Because he wasn't used to seeing his friends on Sundays nobody was likely to visit him. Most of them, anyway, would be out following their own pursuits. All he could hope was that after the match with Beltisham either Keith or Kevin would come round to tell

him how it had gone. Surely, Gary told himself, they'd want to know why he hadn't turned up; they'd sympathize about his injury and he hoped they'd say they'd missed him.

Before setting out for his round of golf Mr Ansell looked into the sitting-room. "Cheer up, lad," he called. "You look like a wet weekend in Blackpool. You'll never get into the rugby fifteen if you can't be cheerful about a twisted ankle. It's all the luck of the game, you know. You have to take the rough tackles with the smooth."

A few moment later it was Mrs Ansell who came in; she glanced at Gary, who was staring out of the window, and then switched off the television set.

"If you're not bothering to watch this it might as well be off," she said. "Have you done your homework yet?"

"You know I have," he said irritably. Homework was all his mother seemed to think of at weekends. "Look, Mum, do you think I could go out for a bit—I mean...."

"Not on your life! If you don't rest that ankle you'll never get to school tomorrow. And I'm not having you missing a lot of school work: I want you to do well at Scale Hill. It's a good school. You've got your future to think of, you know."

The only future Gary wanted to think of was a future playing in the first team for Albion. By that time, of course, Dave Archer would have become a midfield general and therefore Gary could operate as his wing partner. He'd receive so much help and advice from Dave that soon he'd be called up to join the England squad—and then play the game of his life in the World Cup Final against Russia or Brazil.

"So you get as much rest as possible," his mother continued. "It'll do you good to stop thinking about football for a bit."

"I could just manage to go down the road a little way," Gary began without much hope.

"NO!" his mother thundered and swept out of the room.

Gary slumped into a chair, fed up with everything. So deep was his misery that he didn't even hear the next person come into the room. He wouldn't have been very thrilled if he had noticed him. Because there was a difference of nearly six years in their ages he and his brother Ray had very little in common. For one thing, Ray was a big rugby supporter.

"Hey, kid, want to see something good?" Ray asked. He appeared quite excited by something.

"What?" Gary asked without any interest. But he had to say something because Ray was now nudging him.

"Well, keep your voice down—but look at this," Ray whispered.

In his hands he was holding a large plastic box with a transparent lid. So far as Gary could see, all it contained was a lot of soil and a couple of pebbles—oh, and some green leaf-like stuff at one end. With extreme care Ray removed the lid and held the box under Gary's nose.

Gary saw now that the pebbles were actually snails—just common-or-garden snails. He couldn't understand why Ray was so excited about them. In close-up they didn't look quite as nasty as he'd imagined, but there was certainly nothing special about them. Yet Ray was regarding them with the same pleasure as he'd

71

look at a plate of turkey and chips.

"What have you got them for?" Gary asked.

"To win some money with—that's what for,"
Ray replied, much to Gary's amazement. His first
thought was that Ray had gone quietly mad and
nobody had noticed.

"You *what?*" he said (and then remembered
how much his mother said she hated that phrase;
still, she wasn't listening).

"They're *racing* snails," Ray explained. "All
the blokes have them now. It's a great idea. This is
a cracking pair—I've just started training them
and they go like the wind. Well, almost."

"But snails take *days* to get from one end of
the path to the other. I mean, that's about a yard
a week. That's not a *racing* speed."

"You'd be surprised. Listen, Jackie Winters has
got one snail that'll do twelve inches in under
two minutes—that's nearly a record speed. But I
reckon the Ansell Arrow Mark I—that's him,
on the right—will beat that before long. He's
doing pretty well in training. When he's ravenous
and goes flat out for the cabbage I'll have a
world-beater."

Gary was now taking a closer interest in the two snails in the box. Both were on the move, heading for what he now recognized as a scrap of cabbage at the opposite end of the box. To Gary, they were moving at a dreadfully slow speed—at a snail's pace, in fact.

"How do you know which is which?" he asked.

"That's Mark I on the right, his shell's a bit darker than Mark II's. And there's that greyish mark on the crown."

"They look pretty much alike to me," Gary said, adding: "All snails do. So how do you recognize your own in a race if there are a lot of runners?"

"Oh, that's easy. Once you get to know them they're all different. An owner can always pick out his own from among dozens, like men who run greyhounds, you know."

"I'll believe you," Gary grinned, "although thousands wouldn't."

"Look, do you want to see them in action? They're just ready for a spot of training now. They've got to get limbered up for tomorrow night's races at Jackie's place. Come on, let's go upstairs to the training ground."

That was one of the biggest surprises Gary had had so far. The house—and upstairs, at that—was the last place he'd have expected to be used as a place for training snails. Ray was halfway up the stairs before Gary had managed to limp to the sitting-room door and by the time he reached Ray's bedroom everything was ready.

Ray had placed the snails side by side on a narrow, foot-long sheet of glass. For a moment Gary couldn't think where he'd seen it before; then he remembered—and glanced at the dressing-table. That, indeed, was where it had come from; he grinned as he thought of his mother's horrified expression if she could see what was going on. No wonder Ray had told him to lock the door.

At the opposite end of the glass "running track" Ray had put down the scrap of cabbage so that the snails had an objective to reach. He explained that they hadn't been fed for two days and he'd only left the cabbage in the box for a few minutes to get the snails to emerge from their shells.

From his pocket he took a stop-watch and a moment later the race had begun. Gary was fascinated to see that the snails really did seem eager to reach the cabbage and were making slow but steady progress down the track. Ansell Arrow Mark II did veer off course at one stage, but with a gentle push of the finger Ray persuaded him to keep moving in the right direction.

Ansell Arrow Mark I was forging ahead and soon there was no doubt about which one would win the race. Ray kept urging on his favourite with whispers of encouragement and even Gary was becoming quite absorbed by the whole business. He was beginning to realize that snail races might be a lot of fun.

It seemed to have taken rather longer than two-and-a-half minutes for Ansell Arrow Mark I to reach the finishing line, but Ray declared that was what the stopwatch said. He was quite satisfied with his favourite's performance. All the same, he allowed the snail only the merest nibble of cabbage before putting him back in his box. The runner-up he allowed to eat a little more.

"You see, you've got to get them keen on the eve of a race by keeping them hungry," he said. "If they've had a good meal they just go back to sleep—at least, I think that's what they do. And I want to win some money tomorrow night."

"By betting on them, you mean?"

"Yes, we do that all right. But we also have a sweepstake. Each owner puts five pence in the kitty. The winning owner gets seventy-five per cent of the pool and the runner-up gets the rest."

"Have you won much yet?"

"I've only just got this pair, but I'll be in the money before long. Sure of it."

"Do you only feed them on cabbage?"

"No, they like other green stuff as well. I vary the diet. Snails like some odd things. There are some in Norfolk that like postage stamps. They get into country post-boxes you know, the sort that are built into the wall, and when the letters drop through they eat the stamps off them."

Ray was obviously becoming an authority on the subject of snails and Gary was quite happy to listen to him. It had taken his mind off the Sunday Junior League match. It was only when Ray looked at his watch and exclaimed that he had to be off that Gary learned what time it was. At this moment, the match should just be ending.

When Ray had packed his snails away and was starting to change his clothes Gary made his way down the stairs. His ankle was still causing him some trouble, but he thought it was a bit easier. He limped into the sitting-room and crossed to the window. He wanted to catch sight of Kevin and Keith before they saw him. From their faces he should be able to tell whether Bank Vale United had won.

Few people passed along the avenue. Most of the residents, he supposed, were either having an early tea or still reading the Sunday papers. It was another gloomy day and already lights were on in some of the houses. The minutes ticked away, but still there was no sign of members of the team.

By 5.30 he was forced to admit to himself that they weren't coming. They must have gone straight home. What that meant he couldn't be sure. If they'd won they might be celebrating at Keith's house. If they'd lost they probably wouldn't want to talk about the match at the moment; they'd all be so upset. But whatever the result they *ought* to have come and told him about it. After all, he *was* a member of the team.

He spent a wretched evening and in spite of the fact that his family was at home he'd never felt so lonely. When his mother suggested he should have an early night he didn't argue with her. If he was asleep at least he wouldn't be thinking about how his friends had let him down.

Six

Even though he knew he'd have to miss the double sports period at the end of the afternoon Gary was eager to get to school that Monday. There was little chance that he'd see Kevin, who was in a different class, before lunch-time but he just might catch him before school assembled.

His luck was out. There was no sign of Kevin anywhere. So Gary had to fret through geography and maths and chemistry until the bell rang for the end of morning school. Only the fact that he still had to take care because of his sore ankle prevented him from rushing to the dining room. Anxiously he searched for Kevin among the boys in the queues and at the long tables. He had no success. For some reason, Kevin wasn't there. Gary couldn't understand it.

After his meal Gary went up to one of Kevin's class-mates.

"Do you know where Ripley is?" he asked.

"No. He's away today. Don't know why."

That was something he hadn't expected. Kevin was the sort of boy who was never ill. Moreover, he was dead keen on his lessons. He already had ideas about becoming a bank manager when he left school. "If you've got plenty of money you can't go wrong," was his theory. "And banks are never short of money, are they?"

So now Gary had something else to worry about during the afternoon. If Kevin was ill and Gary called at his house Mrs Ripley might not let him see her son. He couldn't very well ask her about the match because she might not know where Kevin went on Sunday afternoons. The only solution was to go and see Keith, but he wasn't sure where Keith lived. He could think of only one way of finding that out—by asking Mrs Ripley to ask Kevin for the address. It was all very difficult.

When Gary went along to the changing-rooms at the start of the sports period Mr Moore immediately asked about his ankle. He seemed quite concerned about it. Gary rolled down his sock to display the bruise. The swelling had almost gone by now but the skin was very discoloured.

"Oh, that's not too bad," Mr Moore said. "It'll soon be back to normal and you'll be jumping about like a flea. You'd better rest it up today, though. Then you'll be fit for Saturday."

"Saturday?" Gary asked, amazed.

"Yes, I'd like to give you a run out with the junior rugby team on Saturday morning. You're a bit young, really, but I talked about it with the Headmaster and he approves. He wants to encourage all the talent we've got for future years. So we'll see how you get on. If it gets tough in the first half, well, we can always pull you off and put somebody else in—that's how we work it in these junior matches. We don't want any boy to overdo it at the start.

"So come and see me at the end of Friday afternoon and I'll check that your ankle's okay. I'm sure it will be."

Gary was too stunned by this news to make

any response at all. Mr Moore seemed to assume that Gary was pleased by this selection for a rugby team and told him he could spend the rest of the afternoon in the library. There was no point in his going out to the sports field when he couldn't take part in a game.

Utterly dismayed, Gary made his way to the library. Few other boys or girls were present and no one interrupted his thoughts. It was obvious now that the school had decided that he was a promising rugby player and so that was to be his game in future. If he did well in this trial he might never be allowed to play soccer again. That was an appalling prospect.

There was, he decided, only one thing to do. He'd have to insist that his ankle was still bad and that he couldn't possibly risk it in a rugby match. Nobody could say it *wasn't* so; only he could know whether it was really painful. Of course, Mr Moore wouldn't like it—he might think Gary was shamming—but that was just too bad. All the same, Gary realized, he didn't want to earn a reputation as a softie; that would be pretty awful.

Now he began to wonder whether perhaps he ought to play, but play badly. If he made a real mess of his game—missing tackles and passes and just running straight into trouble each time he got the ball—then Mr Moore might conclude that he wasn't much of a rugby player after all. So Gary would be dropped for the next match. Yes, that wasn't a bad idea.

Having made up his mind that that was the thing to do he now made the best of his time in the library: he did his homework. Now he could have the evening free to go and see Kevin.

After his tea he persuaded his mother that he was quite fit again. "After all," he told here, "I *did* go to school, didn't I? And I walked home, so I must be all right." That argument was unanswerable.

It was only as he darted across the road on his way to Kevin's, and suffered a twinge of pain from his ankle, that he recalled how his first injury had occurred. It was because he had hesitated on the rugby field; he had been damaged during a tackle and a scuffle for the ball. Might not the same thing happen again on Saturday?

If he allowed himself to run into trouble he might be injured again.

And that could mean that he wouldn't be able to play in the next Sunday Junior League match.

So now he felt as bewildered as he had been when Mr Moore first mentioned the rugby trial. He didn't know what to do for the best. Whichever way he turned, he found problems.

When he rang the bell at Kevin's home it was Mrs Ripley who came to the door. No, she said very firmly, he couldn't see Kevin because Kevin had got tonsillitis. He might have to go into hospital to have his tonsils removed. Gary said he was sorry to hear it, but could Kevin let him have Keith Nash's address. It was very important that he should see Keith. A bit reluctantly Mrs Ripley went to get the address for him. When she returned with the information Gary thanked her very politely and said he hoped Kevin would soon be better.

Gary made no effort to hurry now that he had Keith's address. There was a lot to think about. Kevin's illness would last for at least a week, he supposed, and that meant that Kevin would have to miss the next match. Therefore, he reasoned, he himself was sure of his place in the team. United had few reserves to call on and so Gary would be needed. He was genuinely sorry about Kevin; but, all the same, he was glad that his own position was secure.

The only other problem to be resolved was that of the rugby trial. If he played in that there was bound to be a risk of injury. In any case, his ankle might not stand up to two matches in less than two days. If he were to miss the United game for the second week in succession they might never want him to play for them again. That would be a disaster. So, somehow, he would have to avoid playing in the rugby trial. He went back to the idea of trying to convince the sports master that his ankle was still giving him trouble. He was thankful Mr Moore knew nothing about the Sunday Junior League games.

By the time he reached Keith's home he was feeling in a much better mood. He sensed that everything was going to be all right. Mrs Nash answered the door. She was tall and blonde and seemed, even to Gary, to be very young. Keith, she told him, had piles of homework to do but he should be finished in half-an-hour. Would Gary like to come in and wait? He could have a glass of lemonade if he liked. She was very friendly and Gary went with her into the kitchen.

As soon as she'd given him some lemonade and biscuits she asked him about his interests. Gary was wary about mentioning football in case Mrs Nash didn't know that her son played on Sunday afternoons.

"Don't you play in Keith's football team?" she asked to his great surprise. "I think he's mentioned your name when he's talked about the team. You're all doing very well, aren't you? I must come and watch one day."

Gary was delighted to hear that Keith had talked of him in connection with United. That must mean that he was still in favour. Now he found it very easy to chat with Mrs Nash. He wished his own mother would show as much interest in football. Then he remembered that Keith had said that he always had to go to chapel with his mother on Sunday mornings. At least Gary was spared that.

A few minutes later Keith appeared in the kitchen, carrying a football. He didn't seem particularly pleased to see Gary.

"Oh, hello," he said almost off-handedly. "Thought you'd lost interest in United."

"I thought *you* had forgotten about me," Gary replied.

"That's not a bad idea."

"Now, Keith—that's not a very nice way to welcome a friend," Mrs Nash said quite firmly. "If you're both playing in the same team you should get on with each other better than that. And Gary's just been telling me how keen he is on playing for United."

Keith just raised his eyebrows at that and then jerked his head in the direction of the door. "Come on," he said to Gary, "I need some fresh air." His mother watched them go but she didn't say anything more.

As soon as they were out of sight of the house Keith slipped some bubble-gum into his mouth, but he didn't offer any to Gary. He dropped the ball and then pushed it around with the toe of his shoe. It seemed he was just killing time because he didn't invite Gary to join in any practice.

"Look, I'm sorry about Sunday," Gary said, anxious to have Keith as a friend again. "I just hadn't a hope of playing—this rotten ankle was giving me a lot of trouble."

"Oh?" Keith replied with obvious disbelief. "It was all right on Friday, wasn't it? Kevin saw you kicking a ball about in your road."

Gary hadn't expected that. He tried to explain what had happened when the dog rushed at him but he knew it didn't sound convincing. And Keith didn't look convinced either.

"I reckon you were just sulking because we told you not to be so selfish when you get the ball on the wing. You didn't like that, Ansell, did you? So you didn't bother to turn up on Sunday. You didn't care that we were a man short, did you? That we had all the bad luck going? Oh no, you just took the day off. Well, thanks very much!"

Gary's temper was beginning to rise. In a moment it would explode—hurriedly he started to count up to ten.

It was wretchedly unfair. Keith might be a

first-class player, but he could be surprisingly blind when it came to judging people.

"No, it wasn't like that," he said quietly. "It was as I told you. I'm sorry I couldn't tell you I wouldn't be playing but I wasn't allowed out of the house. What happened on Sunday, Keith? Did we—you—did you win?"

"Lost by the only goal of the match. And we should have had a penalty in the last minute, but the ref wouldn't give it us. They carved Kevin up in the area but the blinking ref just ignored it. Honestly—they should never have let him out of the blind school."

After that outburst Keith's manner wasn't quite so cool, although he kept exploding his bubble-gum as if he was shooting peas at Gary. He agreed that Gary would be needed for the next match, especially now that Kevin was ill. The team had lost its unbeaten record but was still in second place in the League table. On Sunday they would have a chance to go to the top because the leaders were without a game.

"So, if you're not going to turn soft on us again, you can play on the wing as usual—so long as you sling the ball about a bit."

Gary went home much happier than he'd been a couple of hours earlier. He'd said nothing to Keith about the rugby trial because that might only have led to further misunderstandings. Rugby was something he just didn't want to think about.

On Sunday afternoon Gary reached the football pitch on the common several minutes before any other member of the United team. Quickly he stripped off his track-suit and tried a few scoring shots with the ball he'd brought with him. He was in good form, despite a slight feeling of guilt over the rugby trial. Mr Moore had accepted his excuse about the ankle quite good humouredly; Gary would have felt better had he been more difficult. But now was not the time to think about it.

Keith, when he arrived with a couple of the other players, looked very cheerful. He was always at his happiest when he was playing football—just as Gary was. Gary felt they ought to be the best of friends. Instead, it was Kevin with whom Keith was so very pally. They were so different from each other, Kevin and Keith, and yet they'd formed this terrific alliance. When they were together Gary felt excluded: and it was not just because they were older than him. Now, with Kevin missing, he and Keith might get on better.

From the kick-off United went straight into the attack, just as Keith had said they should when he gave them his pre-match pep talk. Park Athletic, their opponents, were not to be allowed to settle down: United planned to go at them all the time to establish a good lead.

All the same, they didn't make much progress. For one thing, Harvey Slater was not acting as the spearhead. Because of Ripley's absence Slater was playing a midfield role, presumably under his captain's orders. Whenever he got the ball he looked for someone to pass to instead of heading for goal. Johnny Butler was a new player at inside-left and he too seemed unwilling to hold on to the ball. Keith was shouting a lot more than he used to do—doubtless because of Kevin's influence in previous games. He kept urging his forwards to shoot, but they were rarely near enough to the goal to do so.

Gary was the first to have a real crack at goal but his effort was easily fisted away by the goal-keeper. Gary knew he should have gone in closer but he feared the defence would fall back too quickly.

At that stage Keith didn't make any comment but his face showed that he wasn't pleased by the failure. Park, perhaps encouraged by that let-off, now began to come more into the game. None of their forwards was very big, but they showed some clever touches. Unluckily for them, their team-mates persisted in lofting the ball down the middle and United's defenders had a big advantage when it came to heading.

Just before half-time, and right against the run of play, Park took the lead. For once Keith him-self was at fault. He slipped badly as he tried to tackle the little winger whom he had completely subdued up to that point. The winger nipped past him and took everybody by surprise when he hit the ball with great force; nobody could have imagined he possessed such a shot. The ball clipped the base of a post but spun into the net. The winger whooped with joy. It was his first goal of the season—but if he continued to hit the ball like that it wouldn't be his last.

Because of his own mistake Keith didn't say much in the interval. On the resumption United scored the equalizer when Johnny Butler suddenly appeared in the penalty area and headed a chipped pass out of the goalkeeper's reach. He had shown great speed to get into position for the header and Keith made much fuss of congratulating him.

The next chance fell to Gary. His speed along the wing also carried him clear of the defence. Unfortunately, none of the other United forwards was upfield when Gary reached the by-line.

Gary had to dribble the ball towards the penalty area, looking round all the time for someone to pass to. Defenders were now coming at him so he moved away from the line, still caressing the ball with his instep. Slater was darting through—but he was too late. A Park player came in behind Gary with a crunching tackle. The boy's heel jarred on Gary's ankle and he almost cried out with the pain. The ball was whipped away from him.

Keith, of course, shouted that he'd been too slow—that he should have gone for goal on his own. Gary was too pained to protest at the unfairness—again!—of the criticism. He could only hobble back to the wing. He'd have liked to have left the field for a bit but that might have looked bad. Gradually the pain receded but he had to move carefully.

United got the winner in the very last minute with another neat goal by Butler. Keith was on top of the world because United were now top of the League. But still he hadn't a good word for Gary.

"I think you're a bit of a softie," he said as they left the field. "But you can play next week if you want because we've got a friendly against a team of girls. That should be right up your street, Ansell."

Seven

Godfrey Ansell, Gary's father, hardly ever spent his Sunday afternoons walking on the common. On this Sunday, however, his golf partner had called off the match and Mr Ansell hadn't been able to fix up a game with anyone else. He didn't mind too much because he had a business problem to sort out in his mind. It was something he preferred to think about in the fresh air rather than at home. It was a lovely crisp and sunny day in late autumn and ideal for walking.

Normally, he wouldn't have shown the slightest interest in the soccer match at the far end of the common. It was only when he got closer to the pitch that he noticed that some of the players were girls. Now he thought he might watch for a bit to see what they were like at soccer. He'd never before heard of the idea of girls playing football.

They were playing a team of young boys—well, he supposed all the players were about the same age: it was just that the girls looked older. They were dressed very neatly in gold shirts and white shorts with striped socks and lightweight boots. Some of them, he saw, could also play very well. They went into a tackle as hard as their opponents and one or two could kick like mules. At the moment it was the girls who were doing most of the attacking.

Several minutes had passed before Mr Ansell noticed that his son was playing in the match. At first, he thought he was seeing things: he couldn't believe it. Then he looked again, hard. He was really quite flabbergasted.

He'd only become aware of Gary's presence when the boy received a good pass out on the wing. He easily rounded the girl who came rushing at him and then made good speed down the flank. A tall, long-haired boy—his hair actually long enough for a girl, Mr Ansell thought—was calling for the ball. Gary judged his centre well and the ball dropped perfectly in front of the long-haired boy, Harvey Slater. The United player controlled it without difficulty, brushed past two defenders and aimed a hard shot at goal. The girl in goal should have caught it but instead she fumbled it. The ball dropped to the ground, bounced once—and Slater rushed it into the net. The United players whooped their delight and rushed to congratulate the scorer. Mr Ansell watched them with distaste as they hugged him (and Gary, he saw, was among them).

Gary was at last beginning to enjoy himself in this match. At the start, he'd taken things too easily, perhaps because they were playing a team of girls. He'd made a mess of a couple of passes because he wasn't concentrating.

In fact, some of the girls were very good indeed. Several times they had come close to scoring. The one thing they were not good at was heading the ball. Few of them even attempted it. Usually they waited for the ball to bounce in front of them and such delays could be fatal. The boys leapt in and swept the ball away from them before the girls could bring it under control.

The real weakness in the side was in goal. Girls were usually good at catching a ball—but not the girl they'd chosen to be their goalkeeper. That, probably, was because she was the last girl to be picked for the match; they had to have *somebody* in goal and so they invited Ginny. And Ginny had thought she was coming along only to watch her friends. Now she was the last line of their defence, and a very feeble line at that.

The sight of Gary had driven Mr Ansell's business problem out of his mind. Of course, he knew only too well how keen Gary was on soccer and he suspected the lad played a few games on the quiet. But he hadn't imagined that Gary was so poor a player that he could take part only in games with girls. That was almost an insult to the Ansell family. He felt quite angry. For two pins, he told himself, he'd order the boy off the field. Certainly he'd tell him a thing or two when the match was over.

It was about this time that Gary noticed his father. The shock was so great it drove all thoughts of the game out of *his* mind. Whatever the reason was for Mr Ansell's presence at the

99

match it wasn't because he'd come to support Bank Vale United. That was certain.

When the ball came across to him Gary was too shaken to trap it properly. It was only at the last moment that he saw it. He lifted his right foot and the ball skidded underneath it and into touch.

One of the girls laughed. Gary felt his face going red. Keith yelled at him to wake up—what did he think he was doing? Head down, Gary trotted into position to mark a girl for the throw-in. The ball was lobbed away in the opposite direction.

Gary glanced across at his father out of the corner of his eye. He could imagine what his father was thinking. He could imagine some of the things his father would say when Gary arrived home that evening. Certainly he couldn't suppose that his father would watch the remainder of the match. The likeliest thing was that Mr Ansell would ban him from ever playing again in a Sunday Junior League match. That was a truly horrible thought; but, he knew, it might happen.

If this, then, was to be his last game for United he would make it a game to remember. He would play his heart out. He would play as he'd never played before. It was the only thing to do.

Gary moved in from the wing in search of the ball. If there were an order from Keith to stay on the wing he would ignore it. Gary was determined to get some goals.

Johnny Butler had the ball in midfield. He dribbled round one girl but another was in his way. Very cleverly, he turned to his left but pushed the ball to his right. It came straight to Gary. Immediately he set off on a weaving run down the centre of the field.

Within a few strides he was well clear of his team-mates—apart from Butler who was running hard down the left wing. A girl came at him with a kind of sideways action; Gary simply shot past her. A few yards further on another defender appeared in front of him. She was moving very quickly. Gary checked, his foot on the ball. The girl slithered past, out of control.

As he picked up speed again Gary could see the goal mouth yawning wide in front of him.

He thought he might exchange passes with Butler on his left. But Johnny gave no sign that he wanted the ball. Gary was free to go for goal on his own.

Perhaps because she'd seen other goalkeepers do it in televised matches, Ginny started to come out of her goal. It should have been to narrow the angle but she really hadn't thought about that. She left a large gap on her left and Gary had no difficulty in sending the ball past her into the net.

Keith was among the first to congratulate him.

"Great goal, Gary boy. Great stuff!" So it was Gary now, not Ansell. Keith was very keen to win by as many goals as possible, for the girls had challenged United to the match. They had been confident they could beat the boys. The following week United were to play a vital League match and Keith wanted his team to get a lot of shooting practice today.

As he trotted back to the centre Gary risked a glance towards his father. Mr Ansell did not appear to have joined in the applause. But another man who was approaching him was clapping very loudly.

Mr Ansell looked round in annoyance—and then saw, to his great surprise, that the newcomer was someone he knew very well. Ted Yates was a man he had played rugby with in his youth and therefore was one of the last people he would have expected to applaud at a soccer match.

"By jove, that was a grand goal," Mr Yates remarked enthusiastically as he came up to Godfrey Ansell. "That boy took his chance like a good 'un. Cool and very clever."

Mr Ansell didn't know what to say, apart from

"Hello, Ted." He couldn't help feeling pleased that it was Gary who was being praised. On the other hand, the boy was playing against a team of girls—so that should be easy. He said so to his friend.

"Maybe," replied Mr Yates. "But some of these girls are almost as good as the boys at soccer. I ought to know—my daughter's one of them."

"*Your* daughter?" That was the biggest surprise Mr Ansell had had so far. It was astonishing to hear that an old rugby pal should allow his daughter to play soccer. It didn't bear thinking about.

"That's right—that blonde girl over there— just got the ball now. Go on, Sally! Take it through—have a shot! You won't score if you don't keep shooting."

Sally Yates seemed to have heard her father's advice. With a very neat body swerve she slipped past Keith Nash—of all players!—and worked her way into the penalty area. With her right foot she hit a hard shot towards the net, but the ball bounced against the crossbar.

"Oh dear," said Ted Yates, with real sorrow,

but no anger. "I keep telling her to keep her foot over the ball, not under it. But she's so eager to score she doesn't always remember. Still, she got herself into a shooting position by her own skill —and that's a good start."

"Do you mean you've been training her?" Mr Ansell inquired.

"Certainly! She loves this game and I want her to do well at it. I think soccer's good for a girl— she can learn a lot about balance and timing and general agility. Sally wants to be a ballet dancer, you know. If she takes a few hard knocks at soccer, well, that's what life's all about, isn't it? Learning how to put up with the rough stuff—it all helps."

"I didn't think you knew anything about soccer."

"Oh, you're wrong there. I had quite a few seasons in the local league after I gave up rugby. I thoroughly enjoyed it—even more than I enjoyed the rugby. Anyway, what about you, Godfrey? You must like soccer as well or you wouldn't be watching this match. Have you got any kids playing here today?"

"Well, I have, actually," Mr Ansell admitted reluctantly. "At least, one of them's mine."

"Oh, which one? A girl, is it?"

"No. That's my son—the one with the ball now. My younger son, Gary."

"What! The lad who scored that goal! My goodness, he's going to get another. Go on, lad, go ON!"

Gary didn't hear that encouragement because he was concentrating on beating his man (or girl, rather); and he didn't need it. He was doing well enough as it was. This time he remained on his wing, taking the ball right along the touch-line but never letting it roll away from him.

A very strongly built girl bumped into him and that almost knocked him out of his stride; to Gary, it felt as if he'd been in collision with a mattress with rocks in it. The girl was Jenny Saxton, the sister of his class-mate Tommy. The referee blew for the foul and Gary himself took the kick.

The ball went to Johnny Butler who held on to it for only a moment before sending a pass back to Gary. Unmarked now, he raced away towards

the edge of the area. The defence was completely disorganized following the free-kick and there was no one between Gary and the goalmouth.

Ginny seemed to have learned her lesson about coming out to narrow the angle. She stayed where she was, her arms spread wide. Gary bored in without reducing speed. For a moment it looked as though he was going to rush into her arms—which would have reduced both teams to laughter.

Gary's thoughts, however, were concerned solely with scoring. Once again he chose his spot and hit the ball with great force all along the ground. Ginny was stranded once more and the ball passed well wide of her to finish up in the very corner of the net.

This time Gary wasn't the only one to be slapped on the back with congratulations. His father received the same treatment from Mr Yates.

"That boy's got a wonderful natural talent— you must be very proud of him," Mr Yates said. He was applauding so enthusiastically that Mr Ansell felt compelled to join in; he realized that for the first time in his life he'd enjoyed seeing a goal scored at soccer.

Gary himself nearly fainted when he saw that his father was actually clapping him. The surprise was as great as if he'd seen Dave Archer turn out for the local rugby club on a Saturday afternoon; it was unbelievable. All the same, he glowed with delight. Now he was determined to score a hat-trick.

"I hope his sports master realizes how good he is," Mr Yates was saying. "Have you discussed his future in the game with him?"

'Well, er, not exactly, Ted—you see, er, well, I mean....'

"Then talk to him tomorrow, man! My goodness, if the scouts from some League club had seen what I've seen they'd be queueing up at your door for his signature when he's old enough to sign for a club. Does his sports master give him enough encouragement?"

"I don't know, Ted," Mr Ansell said unhappily. "Gary doesn't say much about him. I gather the sports master is keener on rugby than on soccer. You see...."

"There's no point in going in for rugby if he's as good as this at soccer. Look, tell me the chap's name and I'll have a word with him myself."

"No, no, there's no need for that, Ted, thanks all the same," Mr Ansell said. "I'll go and have a chat with him. You see, I didn't realize how good Gary was at this game. I haven't really seen him play very often."

"Well, you can't mistake the evidence of your own eyes now, can you? Look, there he goes again."

And, as his father watched with rising enthusiasm and pride, Gary went on to complete his hat-trick.

Eight

Gary was on top of the world. He'd never felt so good as he did now, changing into his soccer kit half-an-hour before the kick-off in United's first Cup-tie of the season. Keith had said he would call for him and they'd go down to the common together, discussing tactics on the way.

As Gary descended the stairs his father came out of the sittting-room and grinned widely at him.

"Best of luck—and I hope you get a dozen goals," he said. "I'll be along there for the kick-off. I'm just doing my books at the moment but I promise you I won't be late."

"Thanks, Dad. See you, then."

Ever since that Monday afternoon a few weeks earlier, when he'd turned up at school to have a chat with the sportsmaster, Mr Ansell had been

Gary's biggest fan. Their talk had worked wonders because Gary no longer had to spend any of his time trying to play rugby.

Mr Moore had been quite co-operative. He'd nothing against soccer himself, it was just the policy of the school to encourage rugby. But if Gary was really keen on the game and not just trying to be awkward, then he would give him some serious coaching.

Mr Ansell was triumphant. Having to fight for Gary had helped to convince him that Ted Yates was right. The boy should do what he was best at and if the school didn't recognize this then it was up to his father to tell them.

Keith rang the bell and Gary opened the door to him. In the past few weeks Keith had become much more friendly. At last, it seemed, he was beginning to recognize Gary's dedication to improving his soccer skills and his value to the team. Of course, Keith was still on good terms with Kevin Ripley, but he didn't spend as much time with him nowadays. Kevin, minus his tonsils, had returned to the team, but it was some time before he recaptured his old form. Possibly because his tonsils had been removed, he wasn't making as much noise either during matches!

It was Gary who suggested that they should call for Kevin on their way to the common and Keith had no objection. Kevin didn't appear at all surprised to see them together; by now he was used to it.

Each boy was aware that the others as well as himself were keyed up for the Cup-tie: it was a match they desperately wanted to win. Each of them was thinking what a great thing it would be if United could win both the League and the Cup in their first season. It was just possible because United had become a very good team indeed. They had confidence in themselves and that counted for a lot.

United had been drawn against Beltisham Wanderers, the only team so far to have beaten them that season. So they had a double incentive to win; besides reaching the second round of the Cup they would avenge that single-goal defeat in the League. That was the match Gary had missed because of his ankle injury.

"I reckon Beltisham will think they're on to a

good thing because they've beaten us once," Keith said as they strolled on to the common. "They'll probably under-estimate us"—it was a phrase he'd read in the sports paper about Albion's opponents in a recent match.

"So we've got to hit 'em hard, right from the start. They may try to take things easy at the beginning, so that's our chance. Right?"

"Right," Gary and Kevin said together—and then grinned at each other.

"You two," Keith added, as they came in sight of the pitch, "keep passing the ball between you —and keep moving up-field. They'll be keeping an eye on Harvey Slater, but that's okay because you won't be giving him the ball. So they'll waste at least one man on marking him. Then...."

Keith's instructions were still in their ears as the players lined up for the kick-off. Because of their success United had attracted a regular and faithful following among their school-mates.

Already the fans were chanting "Uni-TED, Uni-TED!" And then, as the whistle blew for the start of the game, they switched to "In the NET, in the NET." It was a goal that they wanted—and the speed with which it came must have surprised even United's most fanatical supporters.

Slater, following his orders to the letter, quickly transferred the ball to Ripley and then ran hard into the Beltisham half of the field.

Gary didn't remain on his wing a moment longer than was necessary. Moving in-field swiftly, he drew level with Kevin who was controlling the ball as if it was attached to his boots by string. Then, after evading one tackle, he slipped the ball sideways to Gary.

Beltisham, expecting to win the ball in an early tackle, were not bothering to retreat. Their inside-forwards, thinking more about scoring goals themselves than defending, didn't fall back. Gary, switching the ball from foot to foot, made very useful progress before sending a return pass to Kevin. By now the United forwards were at the edge of the penalty area.

Cooke, the tall Beltisham centre-half, was sticking to Harvey Slater like Sellotape. He was sure that Slater, who kept waving his arms about and calling out, was going to receive the ball any moment. Barden, a tough ginger-haired boy who liked to attack instead of defend, made a lunging tackle on Kevin, which Kevin slipped easily. Johnny Butler was racing down his wing and Kevin made as if to pass the ball to him. The Beltisham right-back thought he'd anticipate that move and edged out of the area. Kevin flicked the ball neatly across the danger zone to Gary—who darted forward immediately, completely outpacing his shadow, the left full-back.

Without pausing for a fraction of a moment he hit the ball on the half-volley. It was a superb shot. The ball didn't rise more than a few inches and flew into the net past the motionless goalkeeper.

United had scored before a Beltisham player had even touched the ball.

Their supporters went wild. Leaping up and down on the touchline and behind the Beltisham goal they cheered and yelled— and then again began the glorious chant. "In the *Net*, in the *Net*!" Which was precisely where the ball was. For what seemed like several minutes the Beltisham defenders were too stunned to return the ball to the centre.

The United players themselves were no less thrilled. Gary was nearly smothered by the embraces from his team-mates. But he made sure that Kevin, who had set up the goal, got his share of the congratulations. Gary himself had put the finishing touch to the move, but it had been very much a double-act.

"Right, lads," Keith said jubilantly. "That'll show 'em we mean business this time. Now let's get the second goal."

Godfrey Ansell arrived just in time to see the

ball being kicked off again. His first thought was that the game was just starting—after all, it was still less than a minute after the official kick-off time. The continuing joy of the United supporters soon put him right about that. He felt badly about missing Gary's—and United's—first goal, but he didn't have to wait too long before he could join in the cheering.

Beltisham were clearly so shaken by the instant goal that they were unable to settle down to play their normal game. Their passes were mis-timed or mis-placed, or both, and they were unable to take any grip at all on the match. Having made one bad mistake, their defence soon made another.

Because he'd given them a lot of trouble in the League match Beltisham were still keeping a very close watch on Harvey Slater. United, however, were deliberately not giving him the ball. Harvey knew it was all part of the great tactical plan devised by Keith Nash so he didn't mind. Like every other United player, all that really concerned him was that the team should win.

They knew that one goal was probably not

enough and they were pressing for a second. Butler was also tending to play in the middle of the field with Ripley and Ansell. With Slater wandering out to the wing and Cooke following him the Beltisham defence was badly organized. Gary's confidence that the United forwards would soon find another opening in front of goal was now increasing all the time.

A boy called Buckingham was playing right-half for Beltisham. With Barden and Cooke he made up a middle line that had the initials B, B and C—though not exactly in that order. So, because the trio were the stars of the team, they were always referred to by their supporters as "The BBC." But now with Cooke shadowing Slater all the time, the BBC was completely out of focus for once. Kevin was never out of the picture for Barden was unable to keep him under control. Buckingham, therefore, was at the centre of the defence—but he couldn't do everything on his own.

Barden had made a rash sliding tackle on Kevin and failed to reach the ball. Kevin went round him like a ferret and then whipped the ball across to Gary. As Gary came up to him Buckingham started to retreat, quickly.

That suited Gary. He was still in possession of the ball and he wasn't being slowed down. Just inside the area Buckingham panicked and rushed forward at last to try a tackle. As his opponents came in Gary passed to Kevin who fired a shot at goal. The ball struck the base of a post and bounced back, right to Gary's feet. Without any hesitation Gary slammed it into the net. United 2, Beltisham 0.

Once again Kevin had made the goal and Gary had been in the right spot to score it. This time the boys received an equal amount of congratulations from their team-mates, but no one was happier than Keith Nash. His plan was working perfectly.

Several small boys had rushed on to the field to embrace their heroes. Gary glanced across at his father and saw that Mr Ansell was smiling hugely. He must have forgotten all his old remarks about goal-scorers and silly kids. There was no doubt at all that he was thoroughly enjoying himself. Now that his own career as a sports player was over he could find a new pleasure in Gary's success.

At half-time he had words of encouragement for every member of the team. Keith didn't let them relax for long, however; he insisted that they continued to attack because that was the best form of defence, a theory that wasn't very original but was often followed with good results. The Beltisham players looked downcast and had little to say to each other.

All the same, Beltisham made a good start to the second half. Vidler, their centre-forward, tried a long shot which almost came off for the ball hit the crossbar with the United goalkeeper well out of position.

For several minutes the United defence was under a lot of pressure and Keith Nash was in the thick of the action. His blonde head seemed forever to be nodding the ball away to safety, but not even Keith could prevent the goal that Beltisham scored in the 55th minute. Beltisham had won a corner on the right and Cooke, in the manner of Jackie Charlton, moved into the penalty area.

The winger who took the kick wasn't strong enough to lift the ball very much and it bounced on the edge of the area. Vidler took a swing at it. The ball would have gone well wide of goal but for the fact that Cooke was in the way; automatically he stuck out a leg—and by sheer luck deflected the ball into the net.

Straight from the kick-off Beltisham stormed back into the attack in the hope of getting the equalizer. Both Kevin and Gary dropped back to help their defence, but Keith found a moment to order them to stay upfield. He signalled to Slater to add his height to the United defence, instead; and that was a move that pleased Cooke because it meant he himself could join the Beltisham attack. Ten minutes later he must have wished he hadn't.

Harvey Slater had a very powerful kick and he used it to good effect when the ball came to him. He belted it down the middle and it reached Kevin on the second bounce. Kevin brought the ball under control and went in a straight line for goal at great speed. He was in the penalty area before Burden caught up with him and brought Kevin down with a vicious scything tackle. Penalty!

Dramatically, the referee pointed to the spot. But it was some moments before Kevin recovered from the shaking he'd received when he fell. Keith came up to have a word with him, and then turned to Gary.

"You take the kick," he said. "Kevin's still a bit muzzy and we can't afford to miss this chance. If we get another goal now I reckon we've won."

United's supporters were silent now. Gary gulped at the unexpected responsibility he'd been given. It never occurred to him that if he put the ball in the net he'd have a hat-trick. All he could think of was that United had to win this match.

Carefully he placed the ball on the spot and slowly he walked back five paces. He was going to aim for the right-hand side of the goal. He ran —and hit the ball with the inside of his foot. It hardly rose at all as it entered the net well to the left of the goalkeeper whose dive was much too late.

It was the last goal of the match. Minutes before the final whistle blew the United

supporters had changed their chant from "In the Net" to "We're going to win the Cup, we're going to win the Cup."

Among the loudest of the supporters was Godfrey Ansell.

Also by Michael Hardcastle

UNITED!

'Albion can buy players when they need them. And that's what we've got to do, Keith.'

Kevin Ripley's suggestion staggers the boys – but Bank Vale United have to start winning or they stand no chance of getting the Championship. But buying a player from another team causes more trouble than they anticipate . . .

The second exciting football adventure about the superstars of the Junior League.

Michael Hardcastle

AWAY FROM HOME

Keith can't believe it when he's selected for the Town Boys' Soccer squad. What's more, two of his Bank Vale United team-mates are chosen as well. Then they discover that some of their Sunday League rivals are also in the side . . .

The freedom of playing away from home provides plenty of excitement on and off the pitch.

A Selected List of Fiction from Mammoth

While every effort is made to keep prices low, it is sometimes necessary to increase prices at short notice. Mandarin Paperbacks reserves the right to show new retail prices on covers which may differ from those previously advertised in the text or elsewhere.

The prices shown below were correct at the time of going to press.

☐	7497 0978 2	**Trial of Anna Cotman**	Vivien Alcock £2.5
☐	7497 0712 7	**Under the Enchanter**	Nina Beachcroft £2.5
☐	7497 0106 4	**Rescuing Gloria**	Gillian Cross £2.5
☐	7497 0035 1	**The Animals of Farthing Wood**	Colin Dann £3.5
☐	7497 0613 9	**The Cuckoo Plant**	Adam Ford £3.5
☐	7497 0443 8	**Fast From the Gate**	Michael Hardcastle £1.9
☐	7497 0136 6	**I Am David**	Anne Holm £2.9
☐	7497 0295 8	**First Term**	Mary Hooper £2.95
☐	7497 0033 5	**Lives of Christopher Chant**	Diana Wynne Jones £2.9
☐	7497 0601 5	**The Revenge of Samuel Stokes**	Penelope Lively £2.9
☐	7497 0344 X	**The Haunting**	Margaret Mahy £2.9
☐	7497 0537 X	**Why The Whales Came**	Michael Morpurgo £2.9
☐	7497 0831 8	**The Snow Spider**	Jenny Nimmo £2.9
☐	7497 0992 8	**My Friend Flicka**	Mary O'Hara £2.9
☐	7497 0525 6	**The Message**	Judith O'Neill £2.95
☐	7497 0410 1	**Space Demons**	Gillian Rubinstein £2.5
☐	7497 0151 X	**The Flawed Glass**	Ian Strachan £2.9

All these books are available at your bookshop or newsagent, or can be ordered direct from the publisher. Just tick the titles you want and fill in the form below.

Mandarin Paperbacks, Cash Sales Department, PO Box 11, Falmouth, Cornwall TR10 9EN.

Please send cheque or postal order, no currency, for purchase price quoted and allow the following for postage and packing:

UK including BFPO	£1.00 for the first book, 50p for the second and 30p for each additional book ordered to a maximum charge of £3.00.
Overseas including Eire	£2 for the first book, £1.00 for the second and 50p for each additional book thereafter.

NAME (Block letters) ....

ADDRESS ....

....

☐ I enclose my remittance for ....

☐ I wish to pay by Access/Visa Card Number

Expiry Date